The Alternative

PRAISE FOR *STORYSHARES*

"One of the brightest innovators and game-changers in the education industry."
– Forbes

"Your success in applying research-validated practices to promote literacy serves as a valuable model for other organizations seeking to create evidence-based literacy programs."

- Library of Congress

"We need powerful social and educational innovation, and Storyshares is breaking new ground. The organization addresses critical problems facing our students and teachers. I am excited about the strategies it brings to the collective work of making sure every student has an equal chance in life."
– Teach For America

"Around the world, this is one of the up-and-coming trailblazers changing the landscape of literacy and education."
- International Literacy Association

"It's the perfect idea. There's really nothing like this. I mean wow, this will be a wonderful experience for young people."   - Andrea Davis Pinkney, Executive Director, Scholastic

"Reading for meaning opens opportunities for a lifetime of learning. Providing emerging readers with engaging texts that are designed to offer both challenges and support for each individual will improve their lives for years to come. Storyshares is a wonderful start."
- David Rose, Co-founder of CAST & UDL

The Alternative

Tiffany Jones

STORYSHARES

Story Share, Inc.
New York. Boston. Philadelphia.

Published in the United States by Story Share, Inc.

Storyshares
Story Share, Inc.
24 N. Bryn Mawr Avenue #340
Bryn Mawr, PA 19010-3304
www.storyshares.org

Inspiring reading with a new kind of book.

Interest Level: High School
Grade Level Equivalent: 4.2

9781642611892

Book design by Storyshares

Printed in the United States of America

Storyshares Presents

1

I rested my head against the seat and closed my eyes. I imagined opening them and realizing that this was all a terrible nightmare. The car lurched to a stop and I looked around. This was not a bad dream; it was my new reality. Hot tears filled my sleepy eyes.

"Please don't make me go, Mami," I begged, although I knew it wouldn't work.

"Jade, you know this is where you have to be. It won't be so bad, you'll see."

I didn't say another word. I slipped out of the car and didn't turn around once to look at my mother. I stalked towards the building. Her voice had been full of kindness but I wanted her to feel my hurt.

We had come to South Lake Academy the week before for open house. Everything had been fresh and shiny. Stacks of books sat on the desks in neat piles and smiling teachers leaned in doorframes. But this was not a normal high school. A room at the end of the hall was full of baby cribs and bins of toys. Teen moms and kids who had been booted from regular school went here. And now, so did I. I wasn't exactly booted from regular school, but I had fallen behind in all my classes. My teachers and mom decided it would help if I went here.

The narrow red brick structure was three stories high and rumored to have a basement straight out of a horror film. Today, students lingered at picnic tables or made their way inside.

Keeping my distance, I waited near the portable building that housed the library and pretended to check my phone. It would have been a beautiful morning if I had been somewhere else. I closed my eyes and imagined that I was at the beach like I had been just two weeks before. The air was crisp with fall but the sun was warm on my face. I jumped when I heard the first bell.

This place was much smaller than Carter High, but I checked my schedule to be sure I was right just in case. Inside Mrs. Welling's homeroom I found a seat near the middle and took my first of many glances at the clock.

"Good morning," she said after a few moments. "It's wonderful to see all of you. I see some new faces as well as some very familiar ones."

This drew a few laughs for some reason. I saw a few familiar faces too, but none that I knew well. Mrs. Welling started at the front and had us all tell our name and a little about ourselves. It became clear that the class was made up of students from different grade levels, from freshmen up to seniors.

"I'm Jade, and I guess I'm here to catch up," I said quickly. I noticed the girl next to me give me a brief smil. I tried to smile back.

When it was her turn she said her name was Kimberly and she had started going here the year before.

At lunch, Kimberly walked towards me with a baby boy on her hip. The lunchroom was tiny. Booths lined the walls and there were small tables in the center. I had found an empty one and sipped on my water bottle. I had five dollars but had forgotten there was no real cafeteria here. I was supposed to have packed a lunch, and the snack machines only took coins and dollar bills.

"Aren't you hungry?" Kimberly asked.

She was pretty, with long dark hair, and I could hear in her voice that she probably spoke fluent Spanish. It made me think of my mother, and I felt a pang of guilt as I remembered how I had acted that morning.

I told her I hadn't brought anything and she sat down next to me and offered me half of her food. It was difficult to keep being angry but I didn't stop trying. I was starving, though. My mouth watered as I pulled a chocolate sandwich cookie from its sleeve.

The baby stared at me and for some reason I felt pressured to tell her he was cute. She thanked me and told me his name was Daniel. He really was cute, I thought reluctantly. His chubby face was framed by soft black curls.

After school, my anger bubbled up again as I boarded the bus. I could drive but my mom used her car every day for work and could only drop me off. Carter

High had been just a few blocks away and an easy walk. South Lake was six or so miles from my house but the ride felt like an eternity. The yellow bus seemed faded and rickety. A toddler was bawling in back and I stuck my fingers in my ears.

This is my life? I thought.

The only thing that mattered now was proving that this was not where I belonged.Page Break

2

The first day had been like an orientation. On day two I had an appointment with the guidance counselor, Mr. Lopez. I waited my turn just outside his office until the person before me came out.

"Hello there, Jade," he said, looking at what I guessed was my file. His reading glasses were resting on the tip of his nose. "It looks like you passed your freshman year by the skin of your teeth."

He smiled and looked at me over the top of his glasses. His eyes were smiling too. I shrugged, knowing he was right. The deal had been that I could come to this school or repeat my freshman year at Carter. At least here at South Lake I was a sophomore.

"I see here that you were diagnosed with dyslexia in the fourth grade and that reading seemed to be your main struggle. We've got you in the intensive reading class with Mrs. Welling and I think you'll do well there."

I shrugged again and asked him if there was any possibility of getting transferred back to Carter at the end of the semester. My homeroom and intensive reading teacher Mrs. Welling was nice. I had a desperate hope that she would feel sorry enough for me to promote me quickly. Maybe she would say I didn't even need the class at all.

"We can see how things go," he replied, "and evaluate things in a few weeks. In the meantime, I'm here if you need anything."

I thanked him before leaving, my bubble deflated a bit but not totally flat. As I left his office, I saw a narrow-looking closed door to my left. Something made me reach out and try to turn the knob. It was stiff, locked tight.

"Leave that be, dear," the secretary said, eyeing me from her desk. "No one is allowed in the basement. It's not up to code."

So that was the door to the infamous basement, I thought. At least something in this school had piqued my interest.

* * *

Friday afternoon, I began to feel the relief of having the first week behind me.

"Hold this ball in your hand as you write," Mrs. Welling said quietly.

The item she handed me was a globe about the size of a tennis ball and very squishy.

"Why?" I whispered.

There were only ten or so other students in my intensive reading class. I looked around and saw that two others were holding the same ball.

"Hold it in the opposite hand with which you write. For you, that would be your left since you're right handed. It helps some people focus and also keeps the other side of the brain occupied. I know that sounds weird, but give it a try."

Mrs. Welling was young and acted a little nervous, but she seemed to really want to help. I squeezed the ball as I read the short story and wrote down my answers. Surprisingly it did seem to work. When I was done writing, she read over my answers. She wrote an A at the top of my paper right then and there and I took in a sharp breath.

"Good work, Jade," she said, "Now, look it over for spelling and grammar mistakes."

Spelling and grammar were part of why my grades had been so bad the year before. It felt really good to get credit without being judged for my mistakes.

After school, Kimberly called my name as I was walking to the bus.

"How far away is your house?" she asked when we met up.

I explained where I lived and she offered to give me a ride. I climbed into the front seat of the older SUV. She strapped Daniel into his car seat in back.

"Thank you so much," I said. "That bus is no joke."

Kimberly laughed. "I know, right? I rode it all last year, girl."

She explained that her *abuela* had agreed to help her get a car if she got a part time job and kept straight A's. She had done both and was set to graduate in June with honors. I felt a sight pang of jealousy but then remembered the sleeping kid in back.

I waved goodbye and watched her head back in the same direction we had come from. Kimberly had obviously gone out of her way to help me. I had to admit, I seemed to be getting a lot of that at my new school.

3

It was a pattern now, Kimberly driving me home and me giving her five dollars of my allowance each week. It wasn't much, but I couldn't let her do it for nothing. Today we agreed to study together at my house but ended up flopped on my bed instead. Daniel played on the floor and our backpacks sat untouched in the corner of my room.

"You cheer?" Kimberly asked, eyeing the small trophy on my dresser.

"I used to."

I hated not being on the squad and South Lake didn't offer sports, let alone cheerleading. My first progress report was B's and one C, and I was holding onto the hope of going back to Carter in a few weeks. Maybe I could even try out late and cheer with my friends again this year.

"So are you going to the ice cream social Friday night?" I asked, changing the subject.

"Unless they ask me to work."

She worked at a fast food restaurant and said people were always calling in. That meant she got plenty of requests to work extra hours.

"I guess I will too, then," I replied.

Kimberly was my only close friend at South Lake, and although we clicked, I missed my old friends like crazy. She seemed like she was just moments away from being an adult and I still felt like such a kid. But in other ways we were a lot alike.

The air in my house was thick with the smell of black beans in the slow cooker. Kimberly noticed and said her *abuela* cooked them the same way. We were both the youngest and had an older brother. Hers was already married and mine had just moved out the year before. But unlike me, she lived with both her parents, and her *abuela*, too.

Daniel rubbed his eyes and started fussing.

"I better get home and study," Kimberly said as she rolled off my bed and stretched.

I laughed. "Yeah, we didn't get much done."

After she left, I started the rice and finally studied for the history test we were taking the next day.

When my mami came home she was tired, as always. She kissed my cheek and thanked me because I had dinner ready. Since my brother left, it was just the two of us. When we bumped heads, the house was stiff and silent. But we were getting along, so we listened to each other talk about our day as we ate. I told her about the ice cream social, and she said I could use the car. Now it was my turn to kiss her on the cheek.

* * *

The night of the ice cream social was cold and damp, and eating a frozen treat seemed ridiculous. I hugged myself as I walked from my car to the school cafeteria. I wished I had worn a warm coat instead of a sweater. The windows were squares of yellow light in the otherwise dark campus. It felt like a dream place, familiar but foreign.

Inside, it was warm and I looked around for Kimberly. I hadn't seen her car outside, but hoped I had missed it or she had caught a ride. She hadn't called to tell me she was working so I assumed she would be here.

I pulled my phone out from the back pocket of my jeans. No missed calls or texts. I wandered over to the dessert table and grabbed a paper bowl. There were a couple people ahead of me. I watched Mrs. Welling give them heaping scoops of ice cream.

"So glad you came, Jade. Now what can I get you?"

Three plastic tubs were lined up in front of her, filled with white, pink or brown.

"Chocolate," I said, and then quickly added on a please.

She plopped two scoops into my bowl. I moved down and decided on toppings. I ended up with a big mess topped with whipped cream. I still didn't see Kimberly, but I did see Mr. Lopez.

With nothing else to do, I decided to see if he had some good news for me. The semester would be over in a couple weeks, and I was still holding out hope for the transfer back to Carter. I asked him about it the week before and it seemed he wasn't sure. When I asked Mami, she'd been tired and said we'd talk about it later. I was ready for some answers.

A bright green sprinkle was stuck in his dark mustache and I tried not to stare at it.

"Hello there, Jade," he said, wiping his mouth with a napkin and thankfully removing the sprinkle.

He was on the move, taking his bowl to the trash bin and picking up more along the way. I walked with him.

"I was wondering about getting transferred back to Carter," I said, and then added quickly, "since my grades are up."

"You are doing quite well," he said. "But I don't think you're ready just yet. And your mother, well, she is happy with your progress and wants to see you continue to improve. Let's wait until midyear and see..."

He trailed off and his eyes focused on something behind me. "Excuse me, Jade. I see someone who may not be on their best behavior."

He walked away and left me in my misery. I tossed my bowl of ice cream in the trash and felt the first tear try to escape from my eye. I walked as quickly as I could towards the door and back into the bitter night air.

There was nothing for me inside, no one who understood how trapped I felt. Kimberly had stood me up and it seemed my old friends called less and less. I felt a hiccup in my throat and I walked towards the darkened main building, no idea why. But the side door was unlocked. I closed it quietly behind me. The hall was lit only by the red glow of the exit sign.

Everyone seemed to think that this school was where I belonged, and I had no say at all. The sobs came then and I slid down to the floor and let them. The sound echoed in the empty hall. I felt my phone hit the baseboard as I went down. When I pulled it out of my pocket, I saw that the tiny crack that was already there had grown branches and leaves.

"Great," I said aloud.

I tried to turn it on and nothing happened, other than the battery starting to get hot. It was my mami's old one and didn't hold much of a charge. Now it was probably busted for good. I tossed it to the side, almost throwing it.

No one knows I'm here, I thought.

I was invisible. I was lost but no one knew it. No one was trying to find me.

4

After a few minutes I stood and walked slowly
down the hall. I imagined how my shoes would tap if I
had worn the dressy ones. Instead my tennis shoes
squeaked against the shiny floor. A few emergency lights
made the place look almost romantic. There were no
boys I liked here, no one I could imagine being on this
little adventure with. The skin on my cheeks felt stiff from
the salt my tears had left behind. I was sure my mascara
was all over them too.

In the front office, I looked around. For the first
time I began to feel nervous. I knew I shouldn't be here.

Mr. Lopez's door was shut and so was the one next to it, the door leading to the basement. I twisted the knob and just as I thought, it was still stiff.

This time I leaned into the door a bit and felt it give. I did it harder and heard a little pop. I looked behind me as my heart started pounding. I felt like a stranger in my own skin. I was not someone who broke the rules, but tonight I felt like that didn't matter.

I held onto the doorknob and hit the door as hard as I could with my shoulder. I felt the lock pop loose, and I ran and hid behind the secretary, Ms. Minner's, desk. From there I waited and stared at the black space that the open door revealed.

When I was sure that no one was coming I went back over and peered into the darkness. I checked the doorknob and doorframe and nothing looked broken. I looked down and couldn't see anything but the first two stairs. Feeling along the wall inside, my hand brushed a light switch and I flipped it on.

Now I could see the narrow staircase and a little of the floor below. I took my first steps, keeping my hand against the wall. No railing to hold on to... Ms. Minner was right, this place really wasn't up to code. I pushed the door closed gently, leaving it open just a crack. Getting locked in here would be awful. And it would mean lots of trouble.

Half way down I checked and could still see a little light coming through. I looked again once I reached the bottom, just to be sure.

The stairway was well lit, but the basement itself was dim. The space appeared to be a rectangle with a concrete floor and walls. I could make out shelves lined with boxes along one wall. In a far corner there were stacks of chairs and student desks. Sheets covered what appeared to be large pieces of furniture in the opposite corner.

I took in a deep breath. The air was musty but I relaxed, although a small part of me felt disappointment. This was not a scary place. It was a storage room and nothing more.

I took a step backwards as my eyes adjusted and that was when I felt it; the unmistakable feeling of a hand on my back. In that instant my mouth went dry. I instinctively knew that my phone was still in the hall upstairs. I froze for a second, knowing that I was about to die, or that someone meant to hurt me.

Spinning around to face whoever it was, I felt their hand make its way towards my neck. I screamed louder than I ever thought possible, although the sound seemed to come from someone else.

* * *

Strange blobs of color swam in front of my eyes, and I felt like passing out. But one big, yellow blob seemed so real that I didn't. I focused in on it and saw that it was a tennis ball. It hung from a string and when I looked up I saw that it was attached to a light bulb. I barked out a laugh of relief. This was the hand that had touched my back. I wasn't as brave as I thought I was.

I tugged on the ball and white light flooded the room. I took another deep breath and this time it was shaky. I collapsed onto the sheet-covered couch and closed my eyes. After a few minutes I sneezed from the moldy smell and got back up. I was okay, I told myself. And it was time to go.

But instead of leaving, the writing on one of the boxes caught my eye and I stopped. It was labeled Essay Contest with last school year's date. I pulled it out and my bad luck continued. The box next to it came out too and its contents spilled and then rolled all over the floor. It was a box of squishy, tiny globes. I watched as the floor became covered in small Earth's just like the one Mrs. Welling had given me.

I carried the box of essays back over to the old couch and sat it down next to me.

The first one I pulled out had First Place written on it in black marker. The title was My Future Life. The author was Kimberly Garcia, as in my friend Kimberly. As in the one who didn't show up tonight. As in the one who apparently wrote winning essays.

I was surrounded by what I thought of as reading balls... the small worlds, and I picked one up, then looked back at the essay. The first few sentences grabbed my attention, which was unusual for someone like me who didn't like to read. I could hear Kimberly speak the words as I read them. She was a good writer. I unconsciously squeezed the ball as I read and tucked my legs up under me, settling in.

5

I heard voices just as I was finishing the last paragraph. They sounded far away, probably people leaving the social. My cheeks were covered in tears again, but this time it wasn't out of self-pity. I cleaned up the reading balls and put the boxes away. Kimberly's essay, all ten pages, was folded into a thick square in my pocket. I gave the menacing tennis ball a tug and climbed the stairs. I flipped the lights off up top and carefully closed the door, pulling it tight.

I planned to slip out the same door I had used to come in. I crept down the hall and picked up my broken phone. Through the little window on top of the door I saw a few people out in the courtyard but no one seemed to be looking my way. I crept out and tiptoed away from the building, and that's when I saw Kimberly. Were those police officers she was talking to?

She spotted me, and seconds later she was hugging me and crying.

"Where have you been, Jade? I've been blowing up your phone!" She pulled away and looked at me with wide eyes. I had no idea what to say as things began falling into place. My mother and the cops walked over to me next.

"I don't know if I should smack you or hug you," she said, pulling me to her.

The officer's questions hit me hard. I had to admit that I'd been in the building the whole time. I was a slow reader for sure, but I had no idea that I spent two hours in that basement. Thankfully, Mr. Lopez spoke up when one of the cops asked me if I knew how much trouble I'd caused.

"I think this was a big misunderstanding, officers. Jade was pretty upset and I think I may be partly to blame."

Things cooled down after that and I felt relieved when the police cars drove away. The remaining students slowly dispersed, too.

"Show's over," I thought, feeling like an idiot.

My mother offered to help Mr. Lopez and Mrs. Welling finish cleaning up the cafeteria. They tried to tell her that wasn't necessary, but Mami was stubborn, saying it was the least she could do. That made me feel even worse.

"I got here a little late. I saw your car, and when I didn't see you, I panicked," Kimberly said.

It was just the two of us outside now, both shivering from cold and nerves.

"I figured you weren't coming. I'm so sorry, Kimberly. I didn't know. I didn't know a lot of things."

I pulled the essay out of my pocket and unfolded it.

"Where did you get that?" she asked.

"I found it in a box in the basement. It's far from haunted, by the way," I said. "But why didn't you tell me?"

"You never asked. Plus, it's still really hard to talk about so I never bring it up."

The essay was a story of a future changed forever. When Daniel was just three days old, his father was killed by a drunk driver. So instead of the wedding they had planned for after graduation, Kimberly attended his funeral. I had just assumed he was another deadbeat teenage dad, but I was wrong. He had been working and going to school.

I handed her the paper. She smiled, but it was a sad smile.

"I know you think this place isn't for you, Jade. Maybe you even think it's for losers. I get that. But sometimes the plans change and you have to make the best of them. I'm just trying to do everything possible to make sure that Daniel and I have a good life."

My parents were divorced but I still got to see my dad all the time. I felt awful for Daniel, and Kimberly too.

"You're right. I'm going to put in the hard work for my future. And you're not a loser, Kimberly. Far from it."

My voice broke again, but I was all cried out. We walked arm in arm to the cafeteria. Mami, Mr. Lopez and Mrs. Welling had just about finished cleaning everything up. All the ice cream was gone except for the strawberry. What was left of it had melted.

"Don't throw it out just yet," I said, "I have an idea."

I got two clear plastic cups and poured the softened ice cream into them. Then I topped each with whipped cream.

"Strawberry shakes," I said, and handed one to Kimberly.

"Looks like you salvaged that," Mr. Lopez said, "Good thinking, Jade."

"I decided to make the best of it," I said, taking a sip.

I had to admit, it tasted pretty sweet.

The Alternative

About The Author

Tiffany Jones lives in Central Florida. Writing is her passion and she hopes to one day have one of her books published. The Story Shares contest gave her the opportunity to write a story that she hopes will be an inspiration to others.

About The Publisher

Story Shares is a nonprofit focused on supporting the millions of teens and adults who struggle with reading by creating a new shelf in the library specifically for them. The ever-growing collection features content that is compelling and culturally relevant for teens and adults, yet still readable at a range of lower reading levels.

Story Shares generates content by engaging deeply with writers, bringing together a community to create this new kind of book. With more intriguing and approachable stories to choose from, the teens and adults who have fallen behind are improving their skills and beginning to discover the joy of reading. For more information, visit storyshares.org.

Easy to Read. Hard to Put Down.